EYES IN THE DUST
David Peak

DUNHAMS MANOR PRESS

Dunwich – East Brunswick – Fisherville

Published by Dunhams Manor Press
An imprint of Dynatox Ministries

© 2016 David Peak
Cover art by Alexander Gustafsson.
www.whereisthecreator.blogspot.com

Cover design by Jordan Krall

Dunhams Manor Press
East Brunswick, New Jersey
USA

All rights reserved. No part of this publication may be reproduced, distributed, or transmitted in any form or by any means, including photocopying, recording, or other electronic or mechanical methods, without the prior written permission of the publisher, except in the case of brief quotations embodied in critical reviews and certain other noncommercial uses permitted by copy-right law.

This is a work of fiction. Names, characters, businesses, places, events and incidents are either the products of the author's imagination or used in a fictitious manner. Any resemblance to actual persons, living or dead, or actual events is purely coincidental.

www.dunhamsmanor.com

Second Edition

ISBN-13: 978-1533695253
ISBN-10: 1533695253

Cortland still blamed himself for Claire's death. It was difficult not to. After all, he'd spent an entire weekend badgering her to come with him. He needed someone to help him carry everything necessary to study the region's topography, he said. The fate of his thesis, the term—and therefore his entire scholarship—was at stake. She was right, of course, that the recent hurricane off the coast of Maine had brought on some two or three months of rain in just under a week, a thousand-year storm. The usual footpaths that led up into the hills around Mountain Top Lake would be washed out, the rocks slick, perilous. But he hadn't listened.

For her last day on earth, Claire chose to wear a bright yellow raincoat with matching rubber boots. They didn't have the best grip but they would keep her feet dry. The last thing she wanted, she said, was to spend the entire day with wet socks.

Things started off badly. An entire hour was swallowed by the damp, dark morning when his Jeep got lodged in the muddy, backwoods roads. By the time they began hiking the trail at the base of Eagle Bluff, the sky was a restlessly churning vortex of gilded silver—a series of torrential downpours begrudgingly giving way to oddly beautiful sun-showers. In his bulky pack, Cortland carried the majority of the equipment, his self-leveling surveying instrument, its massive tripod, various binoculars, maps, and GPS devices, while Claire carried the food and water, a high-powered strobe, and heat packs. There was no way Cortland was coming back down without the data he needed to finish his research paper on Maine's glacial moraines.

The first bad omen—in retrospect, so many things looked like bad omens—occurred about halfway up the trail: the rubber treads of Claire's rain boots couldn't get a good grip on the mossy granite and she scraped both of her palms in an attempt to break a particularly nasty fall. "This is stupid," she snarled, her jaw line clenched as she pushed herself back onto her feet. "We shouldn't be up here and you know it." She was right, of course. Trekking up the bluff face, miles away from help, was more than stupid—it was irresponsible. He regretted nothing more than not coming to her side at that moment, holding her in his arms and telling her that he was wrong to keep pushing on, that he was sorry, that they would go home, build a fire, dry up and get warm. But he hadn't done any of that. Instead, he doubled down on his stubbornness. "Are you done throwing your fit?" he said, ignoring the look on her face as she visibly seethed. Now, whenever Cortland thought of her, it was that face he remembered, that awful look of anger and hurt. He couldn't get it out of his head.

There was no way Cortland could have known that those would be some of the last words he ever spoke to her, Claire, the woman he was engaged to marry, the love of his life. There was no way he ever could have known. And so he'd carried on, the petty tyrant leading the way into that disastrous afternoon— the events of which would forever haunt his remaining days.

Even by the impossible standards of global corporations, Applied Logistics was a behemoth, with more than 100 offices spread throughout nearly 40 countries, including all of the world's major economic superpowers. They had their tentacles firmly threaded through everything: financial services, oil, pharmaceuticals. Whatever the industry, as long as it generated cash, some modicum of economic and political influence, Applied Logistics, or the Firm, as they asked to be referred to, had a team of faceless consultants hoteling somewhere nearby, doling out invaluable advice via conference calls and meticulously researched reports. In the few years since Cortland had finished and successfully defended his dissertation—years wasted unhappily as an adjunct professor for various community colleges in small, interchangeable cities—he'd never had any dealings with the Firm. And so it came as quite a surprise when he answered a call from a headhunter with a lucrative assignment: two months in an undisclosed remote area studying what was presumed to be an impact crafter unearthed after the collapse of a cave network, with guaranteed future consultations on the land's mining ops.

This was just the kind of lucky break he'd been dying for. Claire would have scoffed at the notion of being a wonk, writing research at the behest of corporate interests, but this was an offer that was too good to refuse. There was no reason not to accept.

A few days after he'd worked out the paperwork with the headhunter, Cortland sat alone in the luxurious cabin of an Applied Logistics jet. Even for a big-money corporate job, the whole thing was abnormally secretive. They took off from a private airstrip outside DC, after waiting hours for an expected and heavy fog to roll in. Both of his cell phones had been confiscated before takeoff—he was told they'd be returned to him the following morning—apparently as a security precaution. Whoever was calling the shots didn't want Cortland to know where he was going.

Perhaps half a day later they landed in some nameless gray zone in some nameless gray country. Grim-faced soldiers stood motionless along the chain-link fence at the far end of the landing strip. Was he in Poland? He studied their uniforms, made a mental note to look them up later, but forgot about it as soon as a man in a black coat and sunglasses led him to a massive hanger, inside of which was a seaplane. They were taking off in five minutes, the man said.

Again, hours passed. Cortland fell asleep, woke to a smooth landing. The seaplane taxied leisurely before coming to a complete stop, waters rocking it gently. Behind the cockpit door, Cortland discerned the hiss of walkie talkies. Moments later, he was being escorted into a small boat equipped with an outboard motor. The driver was dressed in a black wetsuit, black life-vest, his face obscured by a balaclava. They did not exchange greetings. Cortland was taken swiftly to the shoreline. It was blackest night and the stars were blindingly bright in the limitless sky. There was only a moment to notice the rippled reflection of the moon on the oily dark water, the dense, bristled outline of evergreens atop what appeared to be massive stone formations surrounding the lake, or quarry, whatever it was. The sound of the outboard motor was deafening, echoing back upon itself in a rolling wave.

The belly of the boat ground harshly onto a stony beach. Two men in blue-shirt uniforms—the distinctive Applied Logistics logo emblazoned on their chests—helped Cortland onto land. The boat's driver pushed off and retreated into the night. No time to waste. The sound of the outboard was smaller, softer, now just a whine in the distance. Mag-lites in hand, the two blue-shirts guided Cortland up a winding trail to his cabin, ascending wide spiral risers, talking all the while in heavily accented English, something vague and indiscernibly Eastern European, not allowing him time to think, informing him that although he had no electricity or standardized plumbing, he had gas lamps and a generator-powered water pump, an outhouse, a wood-burning stove, a well-stocked library to help pass the time, that he would have plenty of time in addition to all of the basic amenities, all the food he could ever wish to eat, whatever else it was he had requested on the account's charge code. In the morning, they said, his questions would be answered. He had a meeting scheduled with Mr. Robinson, "the principal" they called him. Until then he'd need to get some sleep. He had a long day ahead of him, lots of work. And then Cortland stood just beyond the threshold to the small cabin, alone, the door clicking shut softly behind him.

His bags had been placed neatly along the wall, cell phones—worthless hunks of plastic without electricity to charge them—placed neatly on the kitchen table. The copper-lined gas lamps pulsed serenely on the wall, giving the cabin a coziness that Cortland found intoxicating. Exhausted, his mind spinning with questions, he kicked off his boots, crossed the room with a few long strides and crashed into the twin bed.

As he fell asleep, he registered a distant humming and wondered, perhaps, if it was some sort of machine working through the night, a rock drill, or perhaps a large generator. It was just a fleeting thought, however, because sleep soon overtook him, submerging him in its warm black flow.

The morning filled the interior of the cabin with radiant sunlight. Cortland fried eggs in a perfectly seasoned cast-iron skillet, brewed luxuriously dark coffee in a glass percolator. He opened a small window over the stainless steel kitchen sink and immediately the smell of pine was everywhere. Again, that odd buzzing noise droned in the distance. It definitely wasn't a machine, he realized. It almost sounded like crickets, but much louder, maybe even cicadas, with barely perceptible undercurrents of—as ridiculous as it might sound—a joyous melody.

Cortland guessed he was somewhere in Siberia, perhaps the Taiga, quite a ways from home, from anywhere, really. Birds called in the distance. The air was thick with humidity and was actually quite sweltering. No wind seemed to penetrate this deep into the forest. After eating his food, he took a few moments to look through the bookcases on the far side of the room, and was surprised to find a carefully curated collection of philosophy, which included numerous works by Spinoza and Leibniz, two of Cortland's major influences. Even more surprising, however, was finding a dog-eared paperback of his dissertation—a slim and nervous book—sandwiched between two much larger, leather-bound books. He pulled the book from the shelf and held it in two hands. *The Nonhuman Turn: Cognition, Decision Making, and Will in Everyday Objects.* Cortland opened the book and flipped through a few pages. Whoever had read through this particular copy had underlined dozens of passages, made copious notes in the margins in handwriting that was largely indecipherable. He returned the book to the shelf. Sure, it had been published by a widely respected university press, but it had gone nowhere, hadn't even secured him a job. He'd been warned that panpsychism would never be taken seriously by academia. An advisor actually took him aside one day and told him that abandoning his empirical studies in geology for such nonsense would be career suicide. But he hadn't wanted anything to do with reality after Claire had passed. He wanted to escape. He knew that his understanding, his intuiting, of the natural world was far more complex than the naysayers could ever fathom. But in the end, it hadn't mattered. His book barely sold fifty copies and was quickly forgotten. The field continued to evolve without him, always new theories gaining traction, supplying the footnotes for even newer theories.

    Dishes soaking in the sink, he packed a leather satchel with a notebook, some binoculars, and a voice recorder, which was issued by the Firm. Out of habit, Cortland took one last look at his personal cell phone. Still no signal. Then he was out the door.

His cabin sat atop a wide, round hill. In the distance, through a pocket of trees, he could see the roofs of perhaps half a dozen cottages; all of them either asphalt shingle or tin. Already sweating from the heat, he made his way down the footpath. He saw now in the daylight that it was the massive roots of surrounding trees that acted as the risers he'd climbed the night before, as elegant and idyllic as any planned public space in any city he'd ever traveled to.

At the entrance to the village, indicated by a crude archway constructed by two birches, a dark-haired boy wearing khaki shorts and an oversized, hand-me-down T-shirt greeted Cortland with a limp wave. He appeared to be a native, perhaps one of the Ket people Cortland remembered reading about in an undergrad sociology class. The boy was barefoot, Cortland noticed, his feet scabby with filth. "You are Mr. Cortland?" he said in shockingly good English. Cortland nodded. "Please follow me. I will take you to the principal. He is expecting you."

Together they walked, the boy moving swiftly and Cortland doing his best to keep up while taking in the surroundings. In the distance, through the trees, sunlight rippled gold on the surface of the water. The cabins they passed were interspersed somewhat irregularly. Dirt footpaths, swept clean of pine needles, had been lined with long, straight tree branches. All of the structures were expertly built, composed of new and expensive materials. They passed through the center of the village, where outdoor cupboards had been built high up in a cluster of trees, their trunks wrapped with sheet metal, no doubt to dissuade bears from finding an easy meal. From there, the path forked, the right side leading into the woods, the left toward yet another tree-root staircase, this one spiraling down toward the stony beach. "Mr. Robinson is there," the boy said, gesturing to a cabin that appeared to be identical to Cortland's.

"This is a very nice village you have here," Cortland said. "Are you from the area?" And then, after it became clear that the boy wasn't going to answer, "What is your name?"

The boy's face was set. "I am told to teach you nothing," he said. "Mr. Robinson will teach you everything. Please go."

Before Cortland had a chance to respond, to ask another question, the door to the cabin swung open, revealing a short, round man in green fatigues. He wore silver-frame glasses and his eyes were small, ringed with dark circles. "Please come in," he said. "I expected you tomorrow. But there's nothing to be done for that now."

Inside, the cabin was a disaster. The kitchen looked as if it hadn't been cleaned in days. Dishes were stacked haphazardly in the sink and the stove was crusted with burned food. Thick black flies buzzed all over everything. The windows were closed, curtains pulled. The shut-in smell was overpowering. In the corner of the room, a shirtless man lay in bed. Big beads of sweat stippled his forehead, ran lines through the caked dust that darkened his face.

"That man has a fever," Cortland said, taking a few decisive steps toward the bed. He saw the man's eyes flutter open and roll up into his head, all bloodshot whites. "Jesus, he must be burning up." Robinson, surprisingly quick, grabbed Cortland by the arm and held tight.

He spoke rapid fire. "Leave him. Please. It's nothing. An insect bite. He was working at the site earlier today and came down with it. Happens all the time here. I've already radioed in for a boat." When Robinson smiled, his teeth large, almost phosphorescent, Cortland got the feeling that it was meant to relax him. It did anything but. "There's no cause for alarm," Robinson said, his voice softer now, controlled. "I must apologize for the state of things around here. I've been at the site for weeks. Haven't had much time for cleaning. And as I said, I was expecting you tomorrow."

"He needs medical attention," Cortland said.

"I'm well aware of that, Mr. Cortland." Robinson pulled a chair from the kitchen table. "Have a seat. You're my guest here, so please make yourself comfortable." He nodded to the man on the bed. "He'll be taken care of in no time at all. You'll see." Again, that phosphorescent smile.

As if to punctuate his statement, the door opened and two men entered. They wore sunglasses and the same Applied Logistics uniforms as Cortland's chaperones from the night before. One of the men, a crooked scar twisting his upper lip, carried a folding stretcher under his arm and the other, his left hand bearing a gaudy gold ring, a first-aid kit. Cortland sat at the table and watched, utterly bewildered. Within minutes, the two men had loaded up their patient onto the stretcher, given him a shot of something that made his breathing noticeably slow, and taken him away. After seeing them out, Robinson took a seat at the table opposite Cortland.

"I do apologize for you having to see that," Robinson said. "I assure you it was merely bad timing. The forest belongs to the insects, you see. It's their kingdom. You should see the clouds of mosquitoes deep in the woods—an ungodly sight. Really something to behold. We are, for the time being, merely intruders in a vacuous world I'm afraid we don't understand. At least not yet." He laughed softly. His face went suddenly serious. "You must have a lot of questions."

Cortland got straight to business. His patience was running thin and he was tired of being kept in the dark. "Let's start with the work site you've referred to." He tossed his satchel onto the table, took out the voice recorder. "I'm told it was a collapsed cave network, but I'd like to hear it from you." He flipped on the recorder. "Tell me why I'm here."

Robinson took his time and explained in great detail. Just over a month ago, a collapse had indeed occurred in an area the locals referred to as Purgatory Gulch, a wide bed of rock that lay between two massive stone outcroppings. These two formations were colloquially known as Heaven and Hell, the former majestic in scale, abundant in plant life, the latter a desolate hunk of blackened rock, long rumored to be the stubborn melt from an impact crater. Apparently those rumors proved true, because the crater uncovered by the collapse was enormous. The fact that the two formations had emerged within a crater in the first place was something of a geological abnormality, a rare natural phenomenon known as "mountains in a moat." Cortland asked for specifics, the approximate year of the impact, the diameter of the crater, whether or not there was present a central peak uplift, any remnants of ejecta. "I'll need to review the field notes," Cortland said. "Everything you've got." It was a reasonable enough request and Robinson agreed to have them delivered to Cortland's cottage, redacted as necessary of course, the following morning.

A few days after the crater had been discovered, Robinson continued, its bottom had fallen out, behaving rather like a sinkhole. This hole had initially been excavated by scouts employed by the Firm's Oil and Gas practice. Although no signs of oil were found, they did discover trace amounts of rich minerals used in the production of advanced electronics, such as smartphones. And so another practice, Energy, Resources, and Minerals, for which Robinson served as the principal, had taken over. The minerals had proved difficult to extract, dangerous even. The hole was seemingly growing deeper by the day. Even the surrounding forest was a threat: new trails had been blazed, the village had been erected, equipment air-lifted in. Perhaps a dozen satellite sites were erected around the perimeter of the crater and complex networks of tunnels were dug into the rock sheet in an effort to create easier access. Significant resources were expended. At first, the Firm had tried conventional mining operations, but these proved unsuccessful. Natives were brought in, easily lured by promises of steady work, free meals, and limitless vodka. "For quite a while," Robinson said, "local labor was as abundant as it was cheap. But lately, we have had little luck persuading the men in the area to accept our offers. They believe something is amiss." He smirked. "Superstitious people that they are. Most have taken to steady drinking to pass the days. Though we have established something of a rapport with one of their elders, who acts as a liaison, tensions are still high. Relations are delicate."

"So why me?" Cortland said, exasperated. "Why bring me out here? I don't have any experience with extractions."

Again, Robinson laughed his soft laugh. "You're not here to oversee the mining operation—in fact all of that has been put on hold indefinitely. The Firm is well informed of this. I write them daily reports on our progress here." He leaned forward, his eyes on the voice recorder. "You're here because of your academic work, plain and simple. What we have here is not something as mundane as a mineral deposit, but rather what I believe to be the basis for an entirely new industry. Imagine for a moment communicating over vast distances without the aid of cellular technology, tapping into the cloud without an Internet connection, downloading entire systems of knowledge in an instant. Absurd, yes? Well, I believe that we have discovered a substance that can make all of that possible. Even more than that. The limit is merely our own imagination. Come, I will show you."

There stood Heaven and Hell, just as Robinson had described them, looming shadowy in the distance. And there, shrouded in the misty low valley enveloping the two great stones, was the hole. The size of it was much larger than Cortland could have imagined, perhaps 30 to 40 meters in radius. It had to have been several thousand million years old. Its shape was divine, a perfect circle—too perfect—with sheer walls of rock face that machines could not have bored more efficiently. He'd never seen a crater look like this before, so precise, so massive. Its blackened depths hatched a magnificent, amorphous cloud of bats. The leathery sound of their erratic flight quickly silenced as they disappeared into the immense sky. Cortland felt robbed of his breath, felt it simply pulled from his body.

"Magnificent, isn't it?" Robinson said, clearly aware of the grandeur of the sight. "Mind your step," he said as Cortland quickly descended the stone-lined footpath. "The trail here can get quite slippery." There's no way Robinson could have meant anything by those words, but they stuck in Cortland's guts like daggers, instantly flooding his memory with visions of Claire, that day at Mountain Top Lake.

Still, he pushed on, pushed away the pain, the principal's voice fading behind him. Cortland followed the path as it arced around the site, slowly descending in elevation as he made his way around, a lazy spiral. Dozens of men—blue-shirts and non-uniformed locals alike—stood near the base of a massive steel scaffold, the size of a small, offshore oil rig, its primary structure scaling at least fifty feet high, elevated on cement pillars firmly embedded in the surrounding rock. The top of the scaffold housed a tower crane, as well as a complex system of jibs, winches, and dozens of tightly coiled steel lines. A few clustered men talked quietly amongst themselves, while others stood alone, stared contemplatively into the crater. As Cortland came close, his boots kicking up clouds of dust in the loose bed of sun-baked dirt spread atop the rock bed, the door to the operator's cockpit snapped open. A tall, wiry man emerged, swung round onto the step ladder, and slid down like a superhero in a comic book, his knees bending slightly on impact. "Mr. Cortland?" he said, betraying a heavy German accent. He stood straight and held out one of his large, gloved hands.

The man was tall, wore tight, black clothing, as well as a light-mounted hardhat and climber's rig. His face was hidden behind a full, reddish-blond beard and aviator's glasses. Before Cortland could take his hand, the man quickly removed the glove from his right hand. "Forgive me," he said. "My hand will be sweaty. We have been working all through the morning." Cortland took the man's hand and shook. He was remarkably strong and his forearm rippled with muscles.

"Preparing for anything?" Cortland asked.

"The platform installation along the chasm," the man said. "It will make unaided descent possible. Finally, after all this time, we can get our equipment down there."

Robinson shuffled up behind Cortland. "I see you've introduced yourself," he said to the German. Then, "Mr. Cortland, please meet our esteemed Mr. Heinrich—one of the world's foremost rock climbers."

"So they say," Heinrich said, smiling warmly at Cortland. "And you are the man who is going to tell us what it is we have down there." He turned slightly and nodded toward the hole.

"You were mentioning equipment," Cortland said, impatience getting the best of him. "I'd like to hear how things have been going so far."

Robinson laughed a little too loudly. "Always cutting to the chase, aren't you?" he said. "All of this will be discussed tonight, over dinner at my cabin. All of this and much more, of course. It is far too sensitive a subject to discuss here." At this, Heinrich merely continued to smile, perhaps humoring Robinson, the reflective silver of his sunglasses glaring beneath the brutal white sun, offering Cortland only an image of himself, red faced and wide eyed. The idea of dining in Robinson's filthy cottage made Cortland's stomach turn. He thought of the bloated black flies, the shut-in smell, that look of anguish he'd seen upon the face of the man who had suffered the insect bite.

"If that is the case," Heinrich said, smearing at the sheen of sweat on his forehead with a dusty forearm, "you must excuse me. I need to head back up to the village and clean up."

Cortland spent the next hour walking the footpath that had been blazed around the perimeter of the hole, always careful to maintain a safe distance from its precipice, accompanied at all times by Robinson. The two men discussed Cortland's work in great detail, Robinson asking many questions, listening carefully. After they had completed the circle, standing once more beneath the tower crane, Cortland saw that the otherwise smooth rock face shattered into a thin, jagged seam. His eyes followed the gash as it widened into a black chasm, disappeared into the depths.

"This was created with strings of explosives," Robinson said, "as well as a pneumatic drill, in order to facilitate the construction of the platforms and their connective stairs. The walls of the hole are simply too sheer otherwise. Structural analysis has ensured that it is quite safe, really. The project will begin in earnest tomorrow." He turned and began making his way toward the path. "Follow me, please."

Cortland took a few steps, then, overcome by a sudden urge, turned and looked out once more upon the horizon. The darkened sun, now a fiery disc, slid behind the tree line, cast the entire valley in purple shadow. There, standing at the edge of the crater, in the sweltering forest heat, Cortland saw something that gave him chills: a woman in a yellow rain coat and matching rubber boots, her face blurry in the distance, a smudge of fleshy color, impossible to make out yet unmistakably Claire's. His hand, as if acting on its own, shot out in her direction, reaching toward her. And then she was gone, disappeared behind a wall of mist. Perhaps the heat was getting to him. Or perhaps he was still exhausted from traveling. Either way, it had been an illusion—had to be. Cortland shook it off, caught up with Robinson, and followed him back up into the village.

Cortland was the last to arrive at Robinson's cottage that night, where, in addition to his host, he was greeted by Heinrich and an old man with dark eyes and dust-caked hair, presumably the native liaison Robinson had mentioned earlier. It was just after sundown, and Cortland was greatly relieved to find that the place had been tidied. Not just tidied, the cottage had been scrubbed spotless. The windows were open, screens fitted carefully into their empty frames. The floor was mopped and polished. A large mosquito net affixed to the ceiling draped over the wide dinner table, where the other men sat. Placed at the table's center was an ornate candelabra, its many arms fitted with rough chunks of blood-red wax. The oily flames provided the only source of light, cast long and crooked shadows that climbed the walls, made the thick netting glow like some kind of carnival tent.

"You remember Mr. Heinrich, of course," Robinson said, handing Cortland a glass of Malbec. "Wine is OK? Good."

Robinson lifted the mosquito netting and gestured for Cortland to take a seat at the table. It was impossible to ignore the fact that Robinson—or Heinrich for that matter—had failed to introduce Cortland to the old man, but before Cortland could do so himself, Heinrich sat down and began making conversation. He appeared rather loose from drinking. His sweat-slicked face gleamed eerily in the candlelight.

Robinson soon joined them and the two men took turns asking Cortland about his flight in, his general impressions of the village, the amenities, whether or not he had yet encountered the mosquitoes en masse. No one mentioned the site, how they had gotten here, what they were doing here. And all the while, the old man sat opposite Cortland and stared, silent. It was unnerving, to say the least, but the talk at the table moved swiftly and, despite his initial uneasiness, Cortland found himself growing more animated, relaxing into the setting. Robinson did well at playing a good host; he laughed at everyone's jokes, made sure that Cortland's wine glass stayed full. Soon enough, the food arrived, wheeled in on trays by one of the natives. The trays contained large platters of smoked fish and hardened loaves of sweet bread.

"We sit here, now, on top of what was once one of the largest, most complex cave networks on the entire planet," Robinson said, ripping loose a chunk of bread with his teeth. He chewed for a moment, slowly rolling the food from one side of his mouth to the other, before continuing. "It is perhaps no coincidence that the forest that surrounds us also contains a veritable constellation of impact craters, some as old as the soil itself. These things are not a coincidence. One informs the other. The seams of life on this planet were ripped open abruptly, exposing the abyss from which all things crawled, and still others wisely stayed behind."

Cortland worried that he'd had too much to drink. The room seemed to swell and sigh with the flicker of the candlelight. The night had been easygoing and fun, but Robinson's tone now was somber, contemplative, even a little bit intense. Cortland looked to the old man across the table, still just sitting there silent, not even eating, watching.

"In the short time that Mr. Heinrich has been with us here," Robinson continued, "I have been unable to answer many of his questions about the site. I lack imagination, creativity. The truth of the matter is that the nature of our work here is unknown, new."

Cortland rubbed his eyes, took another look at the table. Heinrich didn't so much as look flushed with drink as he looked desperate and scared. Robinson's somber words seemed to highlight an undercurrent of melancholy—but for what? It dawned on Cortland that they were isolated here, out in these woods, this forest, miles away from the outside world.

Robinson's grating smile collapsed for perhaps the first time that day, and in its place, a grave look that seemed to suck the air from the room. There followed an unbearable silence, broken only when Cortland again heard the humming in the distance, somewhere out there in all that black beyond the warmth of the candlelight, the safety of the mosquito netting. And hearing that sound again made him realize that it had always been there, that he had somehow tuned it out for the entire day, as if he were getting used to it, like white noise.

"Mankind long ago evacuated the notion of progress," Robinson said, "of evolution. Everything is twisted in time and space—you've written about this very thing, Mr. Cortland. The outside has become the inside. The great wheel will return man to the slime from which he emerged. This is what we really are. The slime molds of your studies exhibiting signs of rational intelligence. Our greatest intellectual pursuits so meaningless in the constant struggle for survival. Life, as we have come to understand it, is composed of nothing more than the elements of infinity, the darkness that corrupts all things."

"I don't know what you mean," Cortland said. "I don't know what any of this means. You're speaking in riddles." The candlelight played tricks with his vision. Robinson's eyes disappeared behind pools of shadow. "If you're referring to the ideas in my book, they're really rather simple. I think that you've misunderstood—"

"Things arrived from outside, which are not us," Robinson said, interrupting, "and these things somehow survived millions of years beneath the surface of our planet. They are inorganic to us, and yet still alive. For these things to decay is to build, to spread darkness is to enlighten. They eat by starving themselves, propagate their species by spreading death. They are the everlasting life that man has unceasingly and so unsuccessfully sought—*being* without thought."

The old man abruptly stood up, his chair legs scraping against the floor. He gave Robinson a stern look before ducking down, disappearing beyond the mosquito net. Cortland again looked to Heinrich; he appeared to be listening to Robinson with the utmost attention, the indoctrinated taking in a sermon. Did he not think this was odd? That Robinson's ravings were those of a madman?

The humming beyond the windows grew louder, millions of crickets chirping all at once, a solid wall of sound. It was as gorgeous as any symphony Cortland had ever heard, seemingly lulling him into some kind of foggy stupor.

Robinson turned his head slightly, brought a single finger to his lips, as if to hush anything Cortland might say, or perhaps even to hush the train of his thought. "Do you hear that? It's the sound of the fabric of all things. They are weaving a new beginning, a new reality." Cortland watched as Heinrich closed his eyes, lowered his head as if in prayer. "Imagine the earth as it was in its earliest stages," Robinson said, "nothing more than a pupa, so many millions of years ago. From vast distances arrives a storm. Sentient stones—the only word our language has for these beings—the building blocks of life, of existence beyond reason—rain from the sky, bursting into flame. They scorch the ground, bury themselves deep beneath the surface of things, slumbering golems, all of them. Above, the ground crumbles back into place, incubating this new life. A life from beyond found not amongst the stars but beneath our very feet. It is here and it has awoken."

Cortland laughed. He couldn't help himself. He was so tired. "You can't be serious. If you're familiar with my work then you'd know that I write about very real things in a very real world, the slime molds you mentioned earlier, for instance, *Physarum polycephalum*. What you're talking about is absurd. Science fiction."

His words seemed to break Robinson's spell. The principal laughed with him. "Of course it is," he said. "Totally absurd. But fun to think about nonetheless. No?" Heinrich joined in on the laughter. Suddenly the pleasant mood of the early evening was restored. Robinson poured Cortland another glass of wine. At this point he was close to polishing off two bottles, no wonder he'd sensed the mood souring—he was wasted. He must have misunderstood Robinson's little soliloquy. That's all it had been: a soliloquy. Talk returned to tall tales and optimism about the prospects of the site. Cortland didn't even notice that the humming had ceased. By the time he'd finished yet another glass of wine he was barely conscious of anything at all.

The canopy of the forest was so thick that even moonlight couldn't penetrate it. He'd borrowed a flashlight from Robinson just to make his way back to his cottage, stumbled after the thin, pale beam as it swept over the twisted trail. He was very drunk. Yet somehow Cortland made it back unharmed, crashed into bed, still wearing his clothes, and became lost in the darkness of the night. Even with his eyes wide open, he couldn't see an inch in front of his face. The night outside was filled with sharp and angular noises that took on a sinister dimension.

He breathed deeply. He was anxious. Somehow the alcohol had energized his system rather than making him feel tired. He took in great heaps of breath in hopes that it would calm him, but only felt as if he were choking on the darkness, his mouth full of ash, grit. The memory of Claire, the regret, coursed through his blood like a poison. He'd been out in the woods for only a day and already he was losing it. He laughed wildly at the thought.

There was always the work. He needed to focus on his work. In the morning he'd review the field notes for the original excavation. Something was off here—that much was obvious.

Something wasn't right with the men at the site, the way so many of them stood around the crater, not talking, blinking. Something definitely wasn't right with Robinson. He'd been out in the woods too long, under too much pressure from the Firm perhaps. Yes, in the morning, he'd review the field notes. That would help. Certainly that would help shine a light on all this madness.

He dreamed about that fateful afternoon at Mountain Top Lake, as he so often did, forever reliving the moments that he could never forget.

The rain had mercifully ceased as they reached the top of Eagle Bluff, though the sky had remained silver, volatile. Cortland set up his equipment as Claire plopped down on one of the wide, flat rocks overlooking the moraine. The view was gorgeous: a steep decline over an outcropping, the vista of a grassy rock bed. A twenty-foot-tall wall of stratified glacial sand and gravel ran the length of one side of the rock bed, its layers a record of the passage of time as the ancient glacier had pushed through the land through sheer force of will.

A few moments later, they shared a lunch of dry tuna sandwiches and carrot sticks. Claire was still fuming over their spat and their conversation was terse, relegated to quick questions and monosyllabic responses. Cortland was too proud to apologize and besides, he knew she'd forgive him easily once they were back in town, laid out on the couch, comfortably eating hot pizza in front of an old black-and-white movie.

Cortland never did fully understand why he did what he did next. Maybe he was trying to get on her good side. Or maybe he just felt the need to say something, anything at all. "There are some bear caves around here," he said. "Up in the rocks over there." He pointed to a slope of granite chunks on the far side of the moraine. "Perfect time of year to check them out, while they're out foraging. You interested?" He asked this fully knowing that she would be. Claire loved any and all animals, loved studying their habitats, their tracks, even their droppings. She was good that way, respected life in all its many forms.

Splayed out on the rocks, her legs crossed beneath her in those big rubber boots, Claire took a hair tie out of her jacket pocket, pulled back her wet, shoulder-length hair into a tight pony tail. The clouds opened for just a moment, letting through a blaze of white sun, its gentle rays illuminating her face. A somewhat crooked smile formed, accentuating the small wrinkle around the corner of her mouth, fine as a thin scar. She was so beautiful it sometimes made him ache. She climbed to her feet. "Lead the way, Ranger Rick," she said.

And so he did. They hadn't gone more than twenty feet before the clouds again formed overhead and unleashed great torrents of rain, as cold as ice—another bad omen if there ever was one.

Despite initially thinking it was going to be impossible, Cortland quickly became accustomed to life in the forest. After his first run-in with a cloud of mosquitos on day two, he'd learned that relative comfort was predicated on thickly applying homemade insect repellent to any and all exposed skin first thing in the morning. The repellent was collected by the natives by smoking birch bark over a metal pan and collecting the tar. The relief it provided was well worth the price of having to go to sleep each night sticky and reeking of smoke.

As promised, Robinson had a few men deliver several heavy boxes of files to Cortland's cottage, the first of many such deliveries. After removing the lid from the first one, which was labeled "Initial findings" in thick black marker, followed by two dates spanning nearly a month, Cortland discovered countless reams of neatly filed reports and correspondence that Robinson had logged with the Firm. Each sheet of paper was a Xerox of another document—the Firm's logo watermarked at the bottom of each page—and was covered margin to margin with tiny, barely legible print. It was going to be a difficult process, but as he'd learned in school, having too much data to work with was vastly preferable to not having enough.

A week or so passed uneventfully. Cortland often ate breakfast at his cabin alone, reviewing paperwork, and shared lunch with Heinrich at Robinson's. There the three men would talk shop. Robinson would fill them in on progress at the crater site, as well as the outlying sites. For instance, the platform installation was nearly completed. Pretty soon, they'd have easy access to the crater bottom. At night the men would get together, play cards, and talk about their various paths in life, whatever it was that had brought them here. Cortland, to his credit, did his best to relay his various theories on sentience in everyday objects, about his theory of how objects did not actually exist in time, but rather essentially radiated time from within, gamely answering any questions the others might have. Needless to say, talk of Cortland's work often resulted in jokes about wise-cracking rocks.

Toward the end of this first week, as Cortland was receiving yet another delivery of the Firm's files, Robinson knocked on his door and asked if the two of them could talk. He looked more tired than ever. Cortland invited him in and the two men sat at the kitchen table.

"Please forgive the intrusion," Robinson said. Cortland gestured as if to say it was no intrusion at all and leaned back in his chair. Robinson continued. "When you first arrived here, you asked why, exactly, you'd been summoned here. I believe I mentioned that the mining operations had been put on hiatus—and that much is true. However, I'm sure you've noticed that we are still digging. Mr. Cortland, I'm going to request that you take a leap of faith and write a recommendation to the Firm that our digging continues, based on your knowledge of our findings. Would you be willing to comply with this request?" As he spoke, Robinson never once took his eyes off of his cup of coffee, which he absentmindedly spun in lazy circles on the table.

"But you haven't told me what these findings are yet," Cortland said. "And I haven't come across anything in the files you've provided me with on which to base such a recommendation. I still have no concept of this substance you continually speak of."

Robinson flashed that phosphorescent smile and stood up. "Very well," he said. "We will retrieve for you a sample from the crater. And this you will use to conduct the research necessary for your recommendation. It is a dangerous procedure, Mr. Cortland. Yet I am sure Mr. Heinrich will be more than happy to descend into the hole first thing tomorrow morning. In the meantime, please begin drafting your letter. I would like to review it upon its completion." And with that, the small man left, slamming the door behind him.

Tendrils of mist rose from the crater behind Heinrich as he stood at its edge, his heavy work boots caked with dust. He was silhouetted by the harsh sunlight, and the steel cables that connected his rig to the winches atop the tower crane made him look otherworldly, as if he had grown tubes that fed into some awful machine. As he explained it to Cortland, the cables—each of which was half-an-inch thick and capable of holding some 30,000 pounds—would lower him into the pit. He tugged on his rig, demonstrating its sturdiness. "There's literally a zero percent chance that anything could go wrong," he said. Heinrich pulled a Firm-issued walkie talkie from a holster near his chest and showed Cortland the channel he'd use to relay his progress.

Cortland asked why Heinrich didn't just use the platforms he had so recently—and with such immense effort—installed along the crater wall.

"It's much faster this way," he said. "Just shooting straight down and then coming straight back up. No problems. But in the event that something unforeseen does happen, I'll let you know—just have them pull me back up to the surface. Only you and Robinson have this channel unlocked because you're the only people here who are authorized to listen in. The technicians are on their own channel. In an emergency, because he is the principal, Robinson is tasked with notifying them."

"OK, we'll see you on the other side," Cortland said.

Heinrich smiled at this. "Always." He raised his arm and gave the thumbs up to whoever was manning the tower crane.

The unmistakable sound of an industrial generator roared to life. A dozen men climbed onto the rig and took positions near control panels, monitoring the cable feeds and winches. The tower crane rotated on its slewing unit so the jib was positioned directly above the seam. Cortland squinted at the operator's cockpit and saw a blue-shirt return Heinrich's thumbs up, his face occluded by massive headphones, sunglasses, and a walkie mic. With no apparent hesitation, Heinrich repelled backward into the crater, cables taut, one of the mechanical arms attached to the tower crane swiveling minutely to track his movement. The generator drowned out any other sounds, echoed throughout the forest, amplified by the wide valley. Looking at those cables, it was impossible for Cortland not to think of puppets, marionettes. And here approached the puppet master now, he thought, sighting Robinson as he exited the path from the village.

As Robinson approached, Cortland saw that a fat black fly was stuck to his face, just beneath his eye. And then that familiar, phosphorescent smile wormed into his features, and the fly, disturbed, took off, the slow buzzing of its flight cutting through the air.

Luckily, Robinson did not stop to talk for long—he was here to oversee the descent, he said, raising his voice above the noise. "Have you written your letter of recommendation yet?" he asked. Cortland shook his head. Robinson, though visibly disappointed, said nothing in return.

Back in his cabin, Cortland picked up his work where he had left off. The reports were finally getting into the nitty gritty, sort of. Any specific mention of rare earth minerals had been redacted, blacked out, but there were still important documents relating to topography and the tracking of astronomical objects. He listened to the crackle of Heinrich's messages over the walkie talkie. Every ten minutes or so he'd relay an update on his depth coordinates, read his oxygen sensor. They really weren't taking any chances, Cortland thought, once more getting lost in the Firm's files, ream after ream of data: contour line diagrams, geological surveys, aerial and satellite images—and yet so much of it was redacted, the smudged pages Xeroxed and re-Xeroxed into oblivion, that he struggled to make any real sense of the information. Increasingly, the documents did not appear to be arranged in any discernible order: handwritten field notes were followed by endless printouts of data, soil readings, geologic compositions, which were then followed by internal comms reports, all protocol and processes, with names and job titles and charge codes redacted. Even the coordinates on all of the satellite images had been blacked out.

An hour or two of this passed, seemingly with no progress. Cortland's temples throbbed with frustration. Heinrich's transmissions continued crackling on the walkie at regular intervals. Robinson chimed in once or twice, giving the go-ahead to continue the descent. How deep *was* this hole?

Cortland felt the whirlwind stress of the past week hit him like a narcotic. He shut his eyes for what felt like the briefest of moments, overcome with fatigue, and was suddenly startled to hear Heinrich cut in on the walkie, shattering the regular rhythm he'd established. "And now the eyes are opening," he said, his voice oddly flat. "I see them now. Eyes in the dust."

At first, Cortland wasn't sure that he'd heard correctly. He picked up his walkie and held the talk button. "This is Cortland. Can you repeat that, please? Over." But there was no response, only silence. "Heinrich? Please respond. Over." He waited for Robinson to demand something similar, waited in vain perhaps, because the silence continued unabated. He looked down at the papers before him and saw a typed report signed by Robinson, dated the day before Cortland had arrived. He quickly scanned the text and was dismayed to read that Robinson claimed the mining operations were not only still active, but remarkably successful. There it was, plainly stated—an absolute lie. He flipped to the next page, which was almost solid black. And yet, something was different about this one: it was squirming. The redacted words and sentences crawled over the page like so many black flies. He cried out, threw the papers onto the table in disgust, stood so suddenly that he threw his chair back onto the floor.

For a few moments, Cortland stood there motionless, his pulse pounding in his neck. He waited for something to move, for the flies to emerge and fill the room.

Heinrich's voice, reptilian with static, sounded once more. "They know everything," he said.

Something inside Cortland broke. He didn't even think twice, simply turned, threw open the door of his cottage and rushed toward the site. He made it about halfway before he came down on an exposed root, actually heard his ankle roll, a wet snapping sound. He tasted dirt as he hit the ground, barely breaking his fall with his elbows. The pain was unbelievable, though it happened in a matter of seconds, and he barely felt any of it. He was back on his feet and limping, thinking only of the sound of Heinrich's voice, the way he sounded so weirdly resigned.

The site came into view, the crater yawning as he fumbled his way down the path, each step rendering the pain more difficult to ignore. Soon enough he saw Robinson, standing near the base of the tower crane. He turned to Cortland as he approached. "Why didn't you say something?" Cortland yelled over the noise of the generator, surprising even himself with how panicked he sounded. "Raise him up," Cortland said, jabbing his finger into Robinson's chest. The other men gathered around them, grumbling amongst themselves, seemingly oblivious that anything had gone wrong.

Robinson stared at Cortland blankly, then licked his lips. "You're covered in dirt, you know," he said. "Like a worm." Then he slowly raised his walkie to his lips and quietly gave the command to raise Heinrich. The winches set in motion. "He went down there at your command," Robinson said. Cortland ignored him, turned his attention to the crater, waited. The wait felt endless. And then Heinrich's rig emerged from the pit, empty, but otherwise undisturbed, as if he'd simply unclipped himself and fallen into oblivion.

Robinson stormed off to his cottage, where he claimed he was not to be disturbed. Cortland, at Robinson's insistence, was carried back to the village on a stretcher by two blue-shirts, his ankle now swollen to twice its normal size. The pain was nearly unbearable, worsened by the grief and confusion he felt over Heinrich's inexplicable decision to remove his harness while dangling above a massive crater.

The blue-shirts took Cortland to some sort of unofficial clinic—a two-room shed that had been outfitted with beds and cabinets filled with medical supplies—where, he quickly realized, he was expected to wrap his own ankle. Cortland retrieved the supplies he needed and sat down on one of the beds. He took a few Tylenol 3s, hoping in vain that they'd be strong enough to curb the pain. The blue-shirts stood on either side of the door, watching him closely. He recognized them: the one with the twisted lip, the other with the gold ring. "You're the same men from before," Cortland said, tearing off a strip of bandage with his teeth. "You tended to the man in Robinson's cottage—the one with the insect bite." The men exchanged a brief look. "Sure," one of them said, "whatever you say."

Just as Cortland finished tightening the compression wrap around his ankle, securing it in place with metal fasteners, his walkie talkie crackled to life and Robinson's voice came through. "Once you've dressed your injuries, report to my cottage," he said.

A few minutes of painful hobbling later, the blue-shirts keeping close watch over him, Cortland pushed open the door to Robinson's cottage and saw the principal sitting at his table, a .45 handgun before him. He looked surprisingly calm, though the colorlessness of his lips, the way his eyes darted from one thing to the next, betrayed worry. "How idiotic can you be?" he said.

"Do you really think that's an appropriate tone to take with me?" Cortland said, bristling. He sat down opposite Robinson, propping up his bad ankle on the next chair. "Especially . . ." He searched for the right words. "Especially considering the circumstances?"

"Heinrich is dead," Robinson said, as if it were a mere matter of fact. "There is no use being indirect with our language. We must be precise. There are problems that need to be immediately dealt with, Mr. Cortland. One word of advice: never, ever reveal that something is amiss before the natives. You should have let me handle that situation. You have no understanding of the damage you've done. They believe a god has been disturbed, that we have set upon a path to destruction.

I told you they were a superstitious people—fatalists—a most dangerous quality to combine with fear." The look on his face suddenly softened. He closed his eyes as if in meditation. "Please, let's not bicker. Not now. It's unprofessional. And we have much work to do."

"That's why you need the gun?" Cortland said, nodding to the handgun on the table. It was solid black and looked immensely heavy.

"When it's called for, of course. It's the natives, they're restless. My liaison has betrayed us, I'm sure of it. Earlier today he and some of the others gathered in the woods beyond the site. They held a clandestine meeting. He is telling lies. He's recruiting. I fear we have lost even more men to the paranoia. He spreads it like a disease. We are dealing with it. I fear for my safety. There have already been threats. Things at the site are chaotic, tense."

"What are you going to do?"

"It's no matter," Robinson said, his eyes cast down toward the table. "If things do really go south, we have a failsafe plan we can put in motion—but only as a last resort. A last resort that you can ensure we avoid. After all, we brought you here from quite a distance, at great expense. I've given you all the paperwork you requested, all of the facts, the research. It's time for you to hold up your end of the agreement."

"Agreement?"

"You need to write the letter of recommendation to the Firm," Robinson demanded, talking through his teeth. "Too much time has already been wasted. The letter must be sent immediately. I've arranged for a pickup. A boat will be arriving any minute. You must tell them what we are dealing with in the crater. And you must promise that it will bring about an entirely new industry."

"But I don't even know that," Cortland said. "How could I? I haven't learned anything since I've been here. The whole time there's been one obfuscation after another."

"That's unacceptable," Robinson said. He slumped in his seat and rubbed each of his temples with two fingers. "Most unacceptable," he muttered.

"Why are you reporting to the Firm that the mining operations for the precious minerals are still active?" Cortland said. "You said yesterday that they had been delayed indefinitely. You're lying to them, stringing them along. Why?"

Robinson laughed quietly then emitted an odd, high-pitched whining sound. He shut his eyes, his open mouth a rictus of frustration, impatience. He raised the gun up over head and shook it, a gesture that, perhaps as intended, made him look totally unhinged. "Included that in the files, did I? I'm sure you understand the difficulty. Creating the paperwork for an entire team of consultants has been difficult. I haven't had much sleep at all."

"Why?" Cortland said. "Why did you do this? Why did you go to all this trouble?"

"Isn't it obvious? Do you really think the Firm would continue to fund this operation of ours if they knew what we were really doing here? I've been buying time, giving them the numbers necessary to maintain our funding. Everything they wanted to hear. All the while, I knew we were getting closer to something that the world had never before imagined possible— unfettered communication. Tapping into the vacuous realm. Don't you see? I didn't understand any of it until I read your work. *The Nonhuman Turn*. There are . . . things down there at the bottom of that crater that are smarter than anything we could possibly imagine. They communicate without using language. They've moved beyond what we know as consciousness. And we are going to learn to harness their intelligence, use it to great benefit. The Firm will grow rich beyond any previous understanding of the word. I will be valorized, promoted to global director. The world will save untold amounts of money. The environment will re-stabilize. Don't you see, Mr. Cortland? We can save the world. We can save all of humankind from its inevitable extinction."

Cortland was dumbstruck. He fumbled for words, to make any sort of response—didn't even know where to start, really. "What sorts of *things* are in the crater?"

"When I first arrived here in the forest," Robinson said, "I discovered that I suffered from a deathly fear of insects, of bugs, spiders, millipedes. Simply stumbling across one of these creatures in my cabin or out on the trail would result in my total paralysis. Such a fear placed me in a rather difficult position, considering their ubiquity." He emphasized the individual syllables of this last word, spitting out each one with contempt. "Forget being mauled by a bear. At least then you have the luxury of dying quickly, relatively speaking. But have you ever seen what the bite of a Karakurt spider can do to a man when hospitalization is not an option? Can you imagine the horror of fresh maggots as they emerge from a man's open wounds? I have seen both of those things—saw them on my very first day here, no less. I soon realized that these creatures inhabit a realm entirely not our own, something you yourself have referred to as the vacuous realm in your writings, the space that seeks only to be filled. This is the nature of the universe, is it not? A hole opens up—somewhere, some place—and pulls in everything that surrounds it. Well, what we have here is a hole, and I believe that it is pulling in our very consciousness. That it is feeding off of us. And that we, in turn, have no choice but to become part of its great black mind. And that by doing so, we can learn from it. Harness it."

"What you're saying is insane," Cortland said.

"Let's not be so reductive. You of all people should be more open minded. They speak to me. They've given me great visions of the way things will come to be beyond time. The beyond itself is a fold within a black dream. You too will come to understand, Mr. Cortland, once you are given to see the eyes in the dust."

Cortland remembered what Heinrich said, just before his transmissions went silent. *I see them now. Eyes in the dust.* Robinson had clearly been driven mad by the immensity and remoteness of the woods, powerful fears he was helpless to control, and theories he couldn't quite grasp. There was no other explanation. It had all coalesced into some kind of sick, twisted fantasy in his mind.

"Don't look at me like that," Robinson said, "with pity in your eyes. You think you understand. You think you know better. But you don't. You are a worm. And it's going to swallow all of us, all of this." He gestured around the room, waving the gun wildly. "I alone can keep it at bay, keep it satisfied. In exchange, we will be granted access to its knowledge. And this knowledge will bring all aspects of life into tune. Surely, you've heard them, Mr. Cortland? The sound of their humming at night? The sound of the fabric of all things? Isn't it joyous?"

An almost unspeakable black horror fell upon Cortland, a veil obscuring any previous understanding of the way things were. Robinson was right; he hadn't even realized it until now. The sound of the humming, the wall of noise, it had long ago melded with his consciousness, tentacles laced through his brainwaves. He knew it to be true.

"I can see it on your face. You *do* know what I'm talking about. You know all too well. But we need more time," Cortland said. "More resources. You must do what I have commanded. It will buy us time. Time is what's most important here. And I fear that we are running dangerously low on this, our most valuable commodity. Now go and do not return unless you have written that fucking letter."

It was midday—the white sun scorching in the empty sky—and the village was eerily quiet, somber. Most of the cottages had shuttered their windows. Cortland limped his way back toward his cabin, his ankle throbbing, the pain so intense that it radiated throughout his entire body, causing even his teeth to ache. The few locals he passed along the way avoided his eyes, didn't even bother with returning his sheepish greetings. There didn't seem to be any blue-shirts around at all. In the village square, he saw the young boy in the T-shirt who had greeted him on his first morning at the site. "Hey," he called out, trying his best to sound anything other than on edge. "Remember me?" Despite his efforts, Cortland undoubtedly sounded panicked. Not that it mattered. The boy didn't even look in his direction, simply turned and fled, the soft thudding of his bare feet on the forest floor bleeding into the rustling of branches as he disappeared into the surrounding woods. Cortland kept on, sucking air through his teeth. Another man, an older native who sat on the ground near the risers, actually snarled at him as he passed, lashed out with a claw-like hand. Cortland barely maneuvered beyond the old man's reach, the sudden movement causing white-hot explosions of pain throughout his leg. The smell of vodka on the man's breath was unmistakable; his half-open eyes looked yellowed and lethargic.

   A flash of yellow in the distance caught his eye. At first he thought, really tried his damnedest to believe, that it was anything else, maybe an exotic bird, or even the sun, the way it so often seemed to glimmer through the trees. But that was just wishful thinking. He knew it was wishful thinking, the mechanism of his mind, trying to protect him from . . . From what? From seeing the impossible? Because what he saw was definitely impossible. The yellow he saw was a dull, mustardy yellow—the yellow of a rain jacket. *Her* rain jacket.

Up until now, Cortland hadn't actually let himself believe that he might be losing his mind. But as he heard himself call out Claire's name, his voice shrill and not at all familiar, not like his voice at all; as he tasted his salty, hot tears; as he crunched down on his ankle again and again and again, he realized that he had probably lost it, was at least sufficiently self-aware enough to know this.

The magnificent trees of the forest enveloped him, darkening the sky, the hot smell of decay filling his senses. Seconds later he came to a small, circular clearing filled with tall ferns, which he parted with his hands as he continued on. Equipment littered the ground and, beyond the center of the clearing, the reinforced entrance to a darkened tunnel emerged from the ground. This must have been one of the satellite sites Robinson had mentioned.

As he made his way toward the tunnel entrance, Cortland nearly stumbled into a knee-deep pit. And in that pit he saw dozens of gray, lifeless bodies heaped on top of another. They'd been stripped of their clothing, some missing limbs, others their heads. The smell was like nothing he had ever encountered before, sweet and rotten at the same time, like apples left out in the sun. And there, on top of all of the others, was the body of the man he'd seen on his very first day at the site, the one who had been bitten by an insect, injected with something, and disappeared from Robinson's cabin. The body had been laid on its back, arms curled tight against the chest in rigor mortis, mouth offset and open. The eyes were gone and a thick centipede emerged from one of the blackened cavities, slid up and around the curve of the skull, its many clicking legs digging into what remained of his blue-gray skin.

Cortland fell onto his hands and knees and threw up everything he held inside, heaving, felt it all come out in one great blackened rope of scabby tissue and yellow bile. His vomit splashed against the ground where it instantly fractured into hundreds of shiny black beetles. The bugs quickly scattered into the recesses of the clearing, racing toward the mouth of the tunnel where they disappeared into the black.

He knew now that she had led him here, Claire had, so that he might learn the truth, in case he had any lingering doubts as to Robinson's monstrous nature. He curled into a ball in the dirt. He was never going home. He would die in these woods. No one who came to Robinson's site ever left, not really. Even the lucky ones, the ones who passed quickly, never fully understanding the sheer magnitude of discovery awaiting those left behind, they were merely absorbed into an endless stretch of cosmic decay.

He felt the first stirrings of everything coming undone, the encroaching black of the hole eating away at the edges of his mind, the vacuous realm, everywhere and nowhere. He turned onto his back and stared into the sky. The white sun trembled, ringed by dozens of crooked black flares, viscous and gleaming, yet swaying rhythmically, weightless like smoke. This was the knowledge: that death was not an exit, but rather a succumbing to the great black folds, those streams of utter ruin that rained down from the spaces between the stars in spidery arcs, falling upon the world and mercilessly wiping it away in all its impermanence, little more than a putrid sprinkling of dust on a quaking bed of volcanic rock.

Cortland shut his eyes and welcomed the all-knowing black as it closed in upon him.

The bear cave was little more than a narrow, crooked passage, and must have been formed millions of years ago when the much larger slabs of granite that composed its angled walls first slid into place. They crouched at its entrance for a minute or two, listening. The smell emanating from the cave's depths was overpowering and earthy. Satisfied that it was unoccupied, Claire shone the strobe into its misty blackness. Gently trickling rivulets of water streamed along the cave walls. Clumps of spongy brown mushrooms sprouted all along the floor.

"I'm gonna go in," Claire said. Cortland's face must have given away his opinion on whether or not he believed this to be a good idea, because she quickly added, "Not too far. Just want to see what it's like. I've never been this close to an actual bear cave before."

The rain was coming down harder than ever, big globs of it, splashing on the rocks, a great wash of white noise crackling like so much static. At this point, Cortland's slicker had soaked through and the cold was seeping into his skin. His teeth actually chattered as he told Claire to be careful, to not go in too deep.

It was a moment that he played and replayed in his memory over and over again, all these years later, a nightmare reel stuck on an endless loop. He watched helplessly as she entered the mouth of the cave, still crouching, carefully inching along the sloping ground, the echoing sound of her boots squeaking against the wet rocks. She pressed her hand against the wall to help her balance, cradled the strobe in her free arm, its beam waving erratically. And then the darkness of the cave seemed to swallow her whole—her bright yellow rain coat disappearing in an instant—leaving in her place nothing but swirling darkness and mist. He heard the unmistakable sound of the strobe's bulb shattering, a soft crunch, impossibly far away.

"Claire?" he called out. "Claire, are you alright?"

The sound of the rain pounding on the surrounding rocks seemed to intensify, a frantic, rhythmic percussion. What if she had been hurt? She could be calling out to him for help and he wouldn't be able to hear her. He called out her name once more, his pulse quickening in his throat. He ducked under the entrance to the cave. And then her voice, or something like her voice, a low tortured groan, coming up from deep below. How had she gone in so deep so quickly?

Cortland got down on his hands and his knees and felt along the ground, quickly confirmed his worst fears: the floor of the cave abruptly gave way to a steep ledge, the rain waters flowing over the slippery edge in a steady stream, pouring into what sounded like a shallow pool some ten feet below. It was too dark to see anything. He called into the blackness.

"I'm here," Claire said. "I . . . hit my head. Freezing. My leg."

What happened next remains in Cortland's memory only as a panicky blur of frustration and agony. There was no way he could have gotten down to her, no way that he could have done anything other than what he did. So why did he still blame himself after all these years? Why did he still feel like he could have saved her if he had only been smart enough, or strong enough to figure it out? Dammit, why hadn't he been able to figure it out?

It took him an hour to get back down to the bottom of the bluff, another thirty minutes to get to his Jeep, which had sank even deeper into the mud. By the time he'd managed to get out onto a main road, flag down a passerby, get on their phone and call for help, another thirty minutes had passed. The sun had gone down and the woods were freezing as he led the rescue team back up to the glacial moraine. And the sun was rising by the time they lifted her out of that cave, the long-awaited end of a thousand-year storm.

She'd been dead for more than twelve hours.

God knows how much time had passed as Cortland lay on his back in that clearing in the woods. The sky above him twirled sickeningly in a time lapse, the light of the stars blurring into glowing arcs of light, as if the world turned one way, the sky the other.

He heard Claire's voice beckon to him, filling him with warmth. "You can still save me," she said. "I'm still right here where you left me. I'm down here at the bottom of this hole." He felt the pain in his ankle melt away, a sudden wave of strength fill his limbs. Her voice was inside him, filling him. "Come and look deep within yourself, look down and deep. The eyes will open for you."

The path back to the village was lined with hundreds of ghastly figures, their skin sloughing from their faces, eyes hollow and obsidian. Among them Cortland recognized the unblinking visage of Heinrich, though the other man made no such human connection. The gaunt specters turned slowly as Cortland passed by, slowly raising their arms and extending their fingers, pointing him in the direction he knew he must travel, toward the center of all things.

Robinson's body—Cortland knew it as such, despite the fact that its face had been degloved—hung suspended by ropes in the birch archway that marked the entrance to the village, a steaming slush of his entrails pooled on the ground below. Placed at the base of each post, like sentinels, were the lifeless corpses of Robinson's two most trusted men: the one with the twisted lip, the other with the gold ring. Their hands had been tied behind their backs, their eyes removed. The old man, Robinson's liaison, stood in the archway, blocking Cortland's path. As Cortland approached, he too stepped aside and raised an arm, pointing. Cortland ducked beneath the gory spectacle, made his way through the village, and then down the path that led into Purgatory Gulch.

There stood the unmovable mounts of Heaven and Hell, black against the pulsing, electric sky. The whole valley was lit with the power of a thousand stars. The two great stones were a gateway to the beyond, Cortland saw that so clearly now. The tower crane rig was gone; in its place stood nothing, a gaping, formidable crag, as if the bedrock surrounding the crater had given way, pulling down the machinery with it, disappearing it into the earth.

Cortland heard the hum, the sound that Robinson had once referred to as the fabric of all things, and knew now that it was emanating from the hole. He listened closely, heard within its drone infinite patterns, genius designs beyond his wildest dreams.

"You always said that once you whittled away all the lies—the illusions—there was only being at its most pure—pure and without thought."

"Claire?" he said. He felt tears streaming down his face, felt the hurt open up, such a deep hole within, aching. He climbed the sharp metal steps that led to the platform system, his boots sounding out loudly on the steel with each step, echoing down into the pit.

"I'm here," she said. Her voice was beautiful, exactly as he had remembered it. "Come to me and our thoughts will be one. We will live together forever."

Time compressed itself into an instant as he made his way down the series of steps and platforms, stretched out once more as he reached the very last platform, its edges licking at the black below. He climbed up onto the steel-beam railing, leaning forward slightly over the abyss. There was no question of belief; things simply were the way they were. He had always known this to be true, an irrefutable fact.

From deep within the swirling black of the pit, Cortland watched as a spot of light hatched in the darkness, a tiny gleam of silver. Moments later, there was another speck of light, and then another. Within the span of a few seconds, thousands more appeared, blinking open in the inky black, all pulling together into a spiral, slowly spinning around a single point, a black disc ringed by blue and purple clouds. The disc slipped away, leaving in its place a hole, a vacuum that needed to be filled, sucking the spiraling clouds downward, their folds lined with the glimmering spots of light, all spinning together so quickly now.

There she was, Claire, at the bottom of the hole in the bear cave. The water from the ledge above showered down upon her, splashed against his yellow rain coat. Her leg was broken, angled oddly. She had pulled back her hood so he could clearly see her face.

"I knew you wouldn't leave me here," she said, extending her hand.

Cortland reached out to her—she wasn't nearly as far away as he had remembered—only registering too late that her voice was not her voice, but the voice of something ancient and greatly displeased. A shadow snaked up from the pit, falling upon him. He was plucked effortlessly from that platform and pulled down into the depths. There was no sensation of falling. Instead, it was as if his body was being carried up into the sky, an endless void stretching up and outward into a perfect cone, the final passage before he could begin a new life among the secretive stars. Such was his last thought before his mortal body was separated into all its various elements, shot outward and all at once into the universe in as many directions as were physically possible.

For G. Winston Hyatt

ABOUT THE AUTHOR

David Peak's writing has been published in *Denver Quarterly*, *3:AM*, *Black Sun Lit*, *Electric Literature*, and *The Collagist*, among others. His book on horror, speculation, and extinction, *The Spectacle of the Void*, was published by Schism Press in 2014. He lives in Chicago where he is slowly working on a novel.

www.dunhamsmanor.com

Printed in Great Britain
by Amazon